THE
INCREDIBLE
THUNDERBIRD

and

Baba Yaga Bony-legs

Retold by MARGARET MAYO
Illustrated by PETER BAILEY

ORCHARD BOOKS

For Natalie
M.M.
With love to the two young whippersnappers,
Oscar and Felix
P.B.

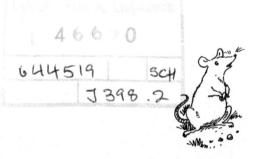

Orchard Books
96 Leonard Street, London EC2A 4XD
Orchard Books Australia
32/45-51 Huntley Street, Alexandria, NSW 2015
The text was first published in Great Britain in the form
of a gift collection called *The Orchard Book of Magical Tales*
and *The Orchard Book of Mythical Birds and Beasts*
illustrated by Jane Ray, in 1993 and 1996
This edition first published in hardback in 2003
First paperback publication in 2004
The Orchard Book of Magical Tales Text © Margaret Mayo 1993
The Orchard Book of Mythical Birds and Beasts Text © Margaret Mayo 1996
Illustrations © Peter Bailey 2003
The rights of Margaret Mayo to be identified as the author
and Peter Bailey to be identified as the illustrator have
been asserted by them in accordance with the
Copyright, Designs and Patents Act, 1988.
A CIP catalogue record for this book is available from the British Library
ISBN 1 84362 084 7 (hardback)
ISBN 1 84362 092 8 (paperback)
1 3 5 7 9 10 8 6 4 2 (hardback)
1 3 5 7 9 10 8 6 4 2 (paperback)
Printed in Great Britain

CONTENTS

THE INCREDIBLE THUNDERBIRD

Everyone is afraid of Thunderbird. Everyone hides if he comes flying overhead. When he flaps his huge wings, thunder booms. He shuts and opens his shiny eyes, and lightning zigzags down to earth. He can strike trees and break them in pieces. He can strike people and they die.

But long ago Thunderbird was even more scary than he is now. In those times he had a *terrible, terrible* habit. He stole beautiful girls. Whenever he saw one, he would just swoop down, pick her up in his long green claws and carry her away to his secret home high in the mountains.

One day, in those long ago times, a brave called Long Arrow and his lovely young wife, Red Flower, were walking beside a river when big black clouds came rolling across the sky. They heard the boom of distant thunder, and rain began to fall. And then they knew that Thunderbird was on his way and they must hide.

They ran towards their camp. They ran and they ran, so fast. But Thunderbird was faster. Soon, there he was, overhead, his wings booming out great deafening thunderclaps, while lightning flashed and sizzled all around.

Thunderbird saw Red Flower, and down he swooped. He picked her up in his long green claws, and off he flew.

Now the powerful lightning had stunned Long Arrow and thrown him to the ground. But he was not dead, and after a while he opened his eyes. The storm was over, and the earth smelt sweet and fresh. But where was his lovely wife? He looked around. There were no footprints. No signs of her leaving. Then he knew Thunderbird had taken her.

Long Arrow was sad. He turned his back on the camp and walked out to the hills, so that he could be alone. Night came, but he did not sleep. He sat, still and silent, on a hillside, and he thought.

By the time the sun rose in the morning sky, Long Arrow had decided what he would do. He strode back to his tepee and filled a soft leather bag with food for a journey. He took his bow and arrows. He said to his family and friends, "Thunderbird has stolen Red Flower. So now I must find the trail to his secret place, high in the mountains, and make him give back my lovely wife."

All his family, all his friends, said the same thing: "Don't go! You can't save her! If you find him, he will surely kill you!"

But Long Arrow
set his mouth firmly
shut, and walked
off towards the
mountains. He
did not know the
trail that led to
Thunderbird's secret
place. He asked every animal he met on
the way to help him – the clever coyote,
the grizzly bear, the far-flying birds and
the fearless wolf.
But none of them
knew the trail.
And they all said
the same thing:
"Turn back!
Don't go! If you
find him, he will
surely kill you!"

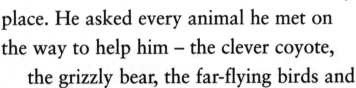

But Long Arrow walked on. He came to the mountains, and still he walked on, until he came to a tepee halfway up the very highest mountain. Raven, the wise one, was standing outside. He greeted the stranger, invited him into his tepee, spread a blanket and offered him food.

When Long Arrow had finished eating, he spoke about his lovely wife and asked Raven, the wise one, if he knew the trail to Thunderbird's secret home.

"You are close," said Raven. "He lives beside the trail that leads to the top of this mountain. His tepee is strange. It isn't made of buffalo skin. It is made of stone, and inside, hanging from the walls, are lots of eyes, two by two. That is where he hides the beautiful girls he has stolen – in these eyes! Only I, Raven, am greater than Thunderbird and have the power to enter his tepee and live."

"I am afraid," said Long Arrow. "Help me, Raven." "Take these," said Raven. "They are strong medicine." And he gave Long Arrow one of his big black feathers and an arrow that had a shaft made of elk horn. "If you point my feather at Thunderbird, he cannot harm you. And if you shoot this arrow through the wall of his tepee, you will have power over him."

"I am still afraid," said Long Arrow.

"So – you don't believe in my strong medicine," said Raven. "Come and I will make you believe." They walked outside and Raven said, "Tell me how far you have travelled."

"I was sad, and I didn't count how many sleeps I had on the way," said Long Arrow. "But the trail was long. The berries on the bushes have grown and ripened since I left."

Raven gave him some ointment and told him to rub it in his eyes and then look back towards his home.

As soon as Long Arrow had done that, he called out, so excited, "I can see my camp! I can see the people, the children, the dogs and even the smoke rising up from the tepees." He turned to Raven and said, "Now I am not afraid."

Long Arrow took Raven's feather and the arrow with the elk-horn shaft and walked along the trail that led to the top of the mountain. Just below the peak, he came to what looked like an enormous tepee. But it was made of stone.

15

Long Arrow entered the tepee, and, though it was very gloomy and dark inside, he could see the shape of Thunderbird, sitting there on the floor. He was huge.

"No one enters my secret place and lives," said Thunderbird, and his eyes began to flash. Then he saw that Long Arrow was pointing Raven's feather towards him. Thunderbird shivered. "You have strong medicine," he said.

"You have stolen my lovely wife, Red Flower," said Long Arrow. "And I have come for her."

"She is mine!" answered Thunderbird. "You cannot have her!"

Long Arrow took his bow and he shot Raven's arrow at the tepee wall. The arrow sped through the stone, making such a large hole that the sun shone in and lit up the place.

Now Long Arrow could see Thunderbird's rainbow-coloured feathers, his curved beak, shiny eyes and long green claws. And he could also see that there were lots of eyes hanging, two by two, from the wall.

"You have Raven's power," said

Thunderbird. "So I must give you what you want. Find your wife and take her."

Long Arrow knew Red Flower's lovely eyes. He lifted the string that held them, and she stood before him…and she was as lovely as ever.

"Do not come again to my people!" said Long Arrow. "We do not want to see or hear you!"

"But you cannot live without me," answered Thunderbird. "I make the storms of spring and summer. I bring the rain that makes the grass green and fills the berries with juice. Without the rain they would shrivel and die."

"Then come and bring us rain," said Long Arrow. 'But promise not to steal our beautiful girls, and try not to harm any of our people with your lightning."

"Take this. It is sacred medicine," said Thunderbird, and gave him a wooden pipe with a long stem that was carved and painted.

20

"When the geese come flying north in spring, you and your people must light the pipe and smoke it and pray to me. And when the smoke rises, I will remember that I must not take your beautiful girls, and that I must try not to harm your people."

Then Long Arrow took Thunderbird's medicine pipe. And he and Red Flower left the secret place, high on the mountain, and walked along the trail that led back to their own camp. There were many sleeps on the way. But it did not seem far, because they were together and content.

This happened long ago. But still, every spring, the people pray to Thunderbird, asking him not to strike any of their people with his lightning. They smoke the medicine pipe, passing it from hand to hand, and the smoke rises softly upwards. And Thunderbird hears their prayers, and he answers them.

A Native American tale

BABA YAGA
BONY-LEGS

Once upon a time, at the edge of a
big dark forest, there lived a girl
called Masha and her father and
stepmother. And that stepmother, well,
when her father was there, she smiled
and spoke sweet as honey. But when her
father was away it was, "Do this, Masha!
Do that!" Whatever Masha did, it was
never good enough. Sharp words were
all she heard.

One day when her father had gone to visit friends in a distant village, her stepmother said, "Tomorrow, Masha, I shall make you a new dress. But first you must go and borrow a needle and thread from my sister who lives in the forest."

"Borrow a needle and thread!" said Masha. She *was* surprised. "There are plenty of needles and a whole lot of thread in the cupboard."

"Don't argue!" said her stepmother. "Just go! And remember to tell my sister I sent you!"

"But how shall I know the way?" asked Masha.

"That's easy," said her stepmother. "Take the path at the back of the house and follow your nose."

Masha was not stupid. She knew her stepmother was trying to get rid of her. Who lived in the forest? Only the wolf... and the bear...*and* Baba Yaga Bony-legs, the old Russian witch. But what could she do? She knew she had to go.

So she combed her golden hair, twisted it into a long thick plait and tied it with a bright red ribbon. Then she asked her stepmother for some food for the journey. Her stepmother gave her a lump of stale bread and a bone with only a tiny scrap of meat left on it. That was all.

25

But Masha took the food and wrapped it in an old cotton kerchief that had belonged to her own mother. And then she set off.

She took the path through the forest, straight ahead. She walked and she walked, one foot in front of the other, until she was so tired she had to sit down on a tree stump and rest.

While she was sitting there, a grey mouse came creeping out from under a bush and sniffed the air.

"You look hungry," said Masha, and
she opened her kerchief, broke off some
breadcrumbs and scattered
them on the ground.
When the mouse
had eaten the
crumbs, he looked
up and said, "Girl with
the golden hair, why are you
walking alone through the dark forest?"

"My stepmother has sent me to borrow
a needle and thread from her sister who
lives in the forest," said Masha.

"Ahhh…" sighed the mouse. "She
is sending you to Baba Yaga
Bony-legs…but you are
a girl with a kind
heart…so don't be
afraid…" He whisked
his tail and was gone.

27

Masha wrapped
the bone and the
rest of the bread
in her kerchief,
and she walked on.

After a while she
came to some birch trees
which grew very close together.

She walked on, and she
came to a clearing in
the forest, and *oh!* in
the middle of the
clearing there was
a hut with staring
windows, perched
on top of two great
chicken's legs. And
the hut was turning
round and round,
round and round.

Masha drew herself up, tall and straight as she could, and she said, "Little house, little house, stand with back to forest and face to me!"

And the hut stood still.

Now there was
a high gate and a
fence of sharp-pointed
stakes around the
clearing, and when Masha
opened the gate it gave a loud C-R-E-A-K!

"Gate," she said, as she closed it behind
her, "you need some oil on your hinges!"

She walked towards the hut and a really
skinny-looking dog came bounding
towards her, barking furiously.

"You look hungry," said
Masha, and she
opened her kerchief,
took out the bone
and gave it to him.
And the dog
stopped barking,
picked up the bone
and set to work on it.

Masha walked on. She stepped into the hut on chicken's legs, and there was Baba Yaga, the old witch herself. She was weaving, and the loom was going *clickety-clack! clickety-clack!* And – my goodness! – she was HUGE, with long bony legs and a mouth full of iron teeth.

"Who are you?" she snarled. "And who sent you?"

"My name is Masha," she answered. "And my stepmother, your sister, sent me to borrow a needle and thread."

"To borrow a needle and thread...*hmmm*...I know what that means!" said Baba Yaga. "Now while I get ready, you must work. Just do the weaving, while I go to the bath house and take a bath. Then it will be time for me to have my supper!" And off she went.

Masha began to weave – *clickety-clack! clickety-clack!* – and after a while a thin black cat came strolling into the house.

"You look hungry," said Masha, and she reached for her kerchief, took out the stale bread and gave it to him.

The cat ate every little bit, and when he had finished, he looked up and said, "This is not a good place to be. You must run away before Baba Yaga returns and eats you with her big iron teeth."

"But surely she will chase me and catch me?" said Masha.

"On the table," said the cat, "there is a comb and an embroidered towel. Take them, and if Baba Yaga catches up with you in the forest, first throw down the towel and then the comb."

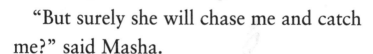

"But what about the weaving? As soon as the clickety-clacking stops, she will be out of the bath house and after me before I can reach the gate."

"I shall do the weaving," said the cat.

"Thank you, good cat," said Masha, and she picked up the towel and the comb. "Now – there is one more thing I must do before I leave." And she picked up a bottle of oil that was standing beside Baba Yaga's lamp.

Meanwhile the cat began to work at the loom. But he had no idea how to weave, and in no time at all he had got the threads twisted and tangled. What a mess and muddle he made of it! But he still kept the loom going *clickety-clack! clickety-clack!*

When Masha stepped out of Baba Yaga's hut, the dog came bounding up to her and licked her hand and wagged his tail.

When she came to the gate, she poured the oil on its hinges. She opened the gate, and it didn't creak. But when she came to the birch trees, they stretched out their branches and caught hold of her and would not let her pass. So Masha undid the ribbon at the bottom of her golden plait and tied a big floppy bow round one of the branches.

35

And the birch trees lifted their branches, rustled their leaves and let Masha pass.

Then she ran – and ran – and ran.

When Baba Yaga came out of the bath house, she heard the loom clacking, so she didn't hurry. She called through the window, "Are you weaving, my little dear?"

"Yes, auntie," replied the cat, trying to talk like Masha. But his voice came out sort of squeaky, and Baba Yaga knew immediately that it was the cat.

She strode into the house, picked up a ladle and flung it at him. "Why did you let Masha leave?" she snarled. "Why didn't you scratch out her eyes?"

The cat curled up his tail, humped up his back and said, "For years and years I have served you, and you've never even given me a burnt crust. But Masha gave me her own bread."

Out went Baba Yaga. Stamp! Stamp!

"Dog, why did you let Masha leave?" she snarled. "Why didn't you bark and bite her?"

The dog looked her straight in the eye and said, "For years and years I have served you, and you've never even given me a dry old bone. But Masha gave me a fresh bone with meat on it."

On went Baba Yaga. Stamp! Stamp!

"Gate, why did you let Masha leave?" she snarled. "Why didn't you creak?"

The gate said, "For years and years I have served you, and you have done nothing for me. But Masha bathed my hinges with oil."

Baba Yaga opened the gate and went through.

Stamp! Stamp!

"Birch trees, why did you let Masha leave?" she snarled. "Why didn't you catch hold of her with your branches?"

The birch trees said, "For years and years we have served you, and you haven't even tied a piece of string on us. But Masha took her own bright ribbon and tied it on a branch."

Then Baba Yaga jumped into her stone mortar, picked up the pestle and, using it to drive her forward, she was off, through the forest...*whoo-oosh!*

As soon as Masha heard the noise, she looked back, and when she saw Baba Yaga on the path behind her, she threw down the towel. And there sprang up a great wide river, brimful of water.

Baba Yaga's mortar was too heavy
to float across, so she turned back. She
found her cattle, drove them to the river
and they drank and drank, until the
water was gone. Then she was on her
way again...*whoo-oosh!*

Masha heard the noise, and when she saw Baba Yaga coming, she threw down the comb. And there sprang up a great host of tall trees, hundreds and thousands of them, so close together it would have been hard for a fly to creep between.

Baba Yaga sharpened her iron teeth. She bit into a tree and hurled it aside. She sharpened her teeth, bit into another tree and hurled it aside.

On and on she went. Sharpening, biting and hurling. But the trees were so many and so close that she could not get through. In the end, shouting and snarling, she turned round and went home.

And Masha? Well, she ran – and ran – and ran.

It was almost dark by the time she got to the edge of the forest. The lamps were lit in her house, and her father was standing outside, looking for her.

"Where have you been?" he called out when he saw her. "What happened? I have been looking for you everywhere."

Masha answered, "Stepmother sent me to her own sister in the forest to borrow a needle and thread, and that sister was Baba Yaga Bony-legs, the witch. It was hard to escape. But some friends helped me, and I managed at last."

When her father heard this, he was angry and strode into the house. But her stepmother had gone.

She had seen Masha and heard everything. She knew she had been found out, and had run off into the forest. And whether she reached the house of her sister, Baba Yaga Bony-legs – or whether the wolf or the bear got her first – no one ever knew.

So that was that. Masha and her father never saw her again. And, from that time on, they lived together in peace and contentment, in their house at the edge of the big dark forest.

A Russian tale

THE INCREDIBLE THUNDERBIRD

A Native American Tale

Across North America the idea that thunder was the sound of a bird flapping its wings, and that lightning flashed when it blinked its eyes, was widespread among Native American tribes. Some thought there was a flock of thunderbirds. Others – like the Blackfeet of the northern plains, who told this tale – thought there was just the one enormous bird.

In *The Incredible Thunderbird*, Long Arrow is very afraid of Thunderbird, but he is brave and determined to rescue his lovely wife. Yet in the end, without the help of Raven's 'strong medicine', he would have been powerless. The Blackfeet were renowned for making exceptionally beautiful pipes. They held solemn ceremonies, as in this tale, when they smoked and prayed to the great spirits. So Thunderbird's gift of a pipe shows the seriousness of his promise.

In the days before scientists understood about thunder and lightning, people made up different explanations. The Scandinavian Vikings imagined that thunder might be the rumble of their god Thor's shiny chariot, as he raced across the sky.

BABA YAGA BONY-LEGS

A Russian Tale

No other country has a witch in its stories quite like the Russian Baba Yaga, with her iron teeth, bony legs and hut that spins round and round on its chicken legs. But like the witch in the German story, *Hansel and Gretel*, she does live in a forest, in an unusual house and she eats children.

Masha, the heroine in *Baba Yaga Bony-legs*, has a kind heart. This is what saves her, exactly as the mouse promises it will. She gives the very last of her food to the mouse, dog and cat. Even when she is running for her life she stops to oil the creaky gate and ties her bright ribbon on a tree. In return, the cat, dog, gate and trees all do something to help Masha. But without the cat's magic gifts of a comb and towel, Baba Yaga would have caught her.

In *Hansel and Gretel* the children escape from the witch without the help of magic. They are clever and cunning and manage to trick the witch. In both stories, however, the children may be scared, but they don't give up. Once free, they find the way home and then live happily ever after with their fathers.

MAGICAL TALES
from
AROUND THE WORLD

Retold by Margaret Mayo ✳ Illustrated by Peter Bailey

Orchard Myths are available from all good bookshops,
or can be ordered direct from the publisher:
Orchard Books, PO BOX 29, Douglas IM99 1BQ
Credit card orders please telephone 01624 836000
or fax 01624 837033
or e-mail: bookshop@enterprise.net for details.

To order please quote title, author and ISBN
and your full name and address.
Cheques and postal orders should be
made payable to 'Bookpost plc'.
Postage and packing is FREE within the UK
(overseas customers should add £1.00 per book).

Prices and availability are subject to change.